Birds in Bras

Breasted, Chested, Boobies & Tits

© 2019 Cathy Comora
Publisher: MAGICAL GENIE, LLC
Parsippany, NJ 07054
Birds in Bras:
Breasted, Chested, Boobies & Tits
ISBN-13: 978-0-578-46083-3
Photos: Shutterstock

www.birdsinbras.com

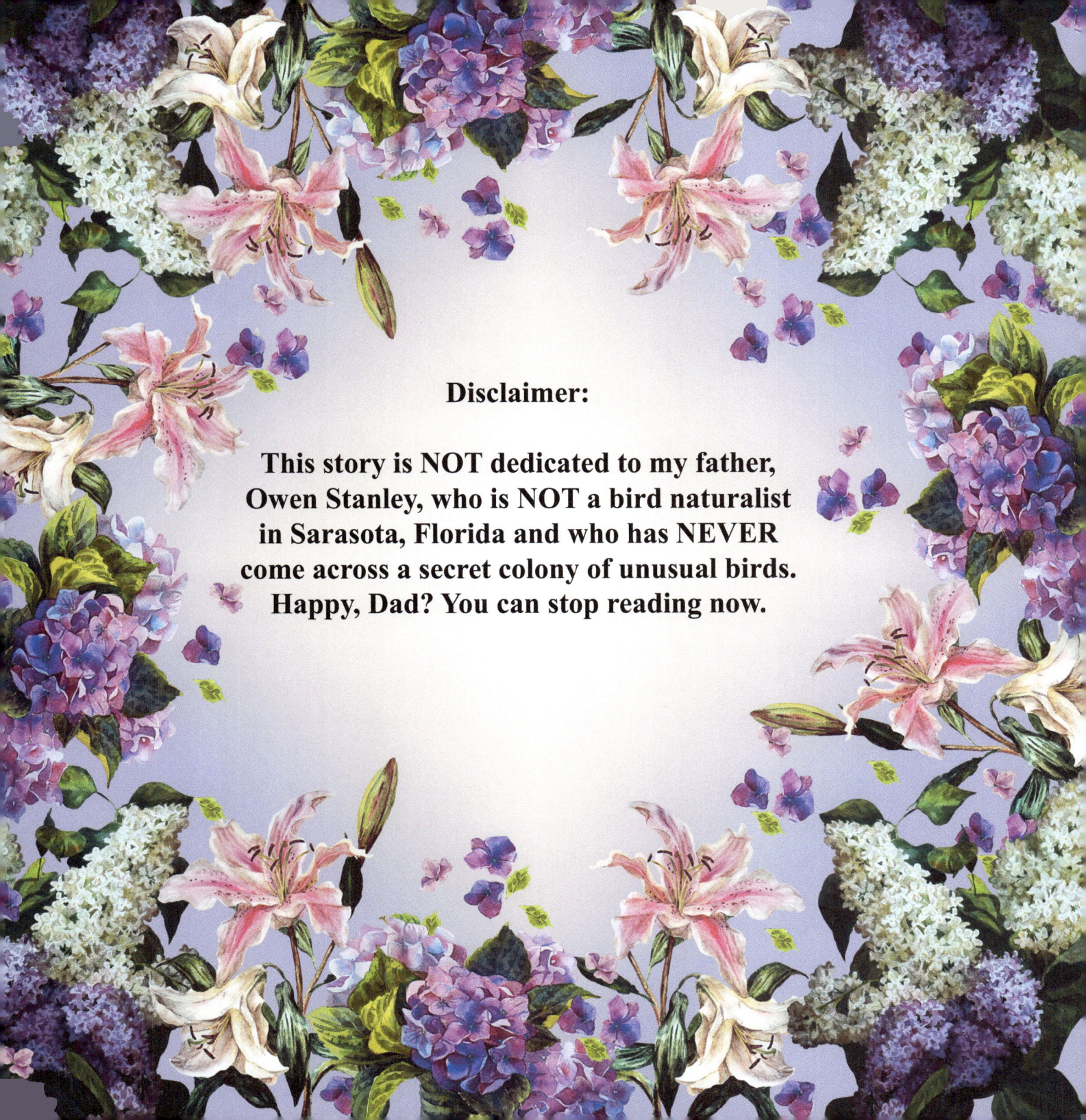

Disclaimer:

This story is NOT dedicated to my father, Owen Stanley, who is NOT a bird naturalist in Sarasota, Florida and who has NEVER come across a secret colony of unusual birds. Happy, Dad? You can stop reading now.

Birds in Bras:
Breasted, Chested, Boobies & Tits

My father, Owen Stanley, a bird naturalist in Sarasota, Florida, has found a secret colony of birds that he doesn't want me to tell you about. Why? He's afraid that if word gets out it might attract a weirdo element to the local bird watching community. (Like that could ever happen!)

Here's what did happen, I recently moved from New Jersey to Sarasota, Florida. Early one summer morning, my father called to ask me if I would like to go owl-watching at Pinecraft Park. I said, "Sure." I had never seen an owl in its natural habitat, and I also wanted to see Pinecraft Park, which I knew was in the Amish Pinecraft Village community. I figured I could kill two birds with one scone! (A little Amish humor.)

My father picked me up at 8 a.m. and off we drove to Pinecraft Park. It was only a ten-minute ride and my father used the time to regale me with an abbreviated version of his Owling 101: "Who Gives a Hoot" presentation, usually reserved for paying participants in his birdwatching classes.

Before I knew it, we were pulling into the Pinecraft Park parking lot. "Let's get to owling!" I cried, but before I could touch the door handle, I heard the automatic doors lock. "Dad, you've got to unlock the doors," I said. Silence. I looked over at my father, who was suddenly quiet, which if you knew my father, you'd know is cause for alarm.

He looked at me and said, "Cathy, I have to tell you something. You cannot tell anyone what I am about to tell you."

"Ok. What is it?"

"Do you promise?" he asked insistently.

"Yes, I promise!" I answered emphatically.

"Let me see your hands!" he demanded.

Dang! I thought, as I uncrossed my fingers and brought them out from behind my back.

"What about your toes?" he asked suspiciously.

"They're uncrossed! I swear – jeez – ye of little faith!" I said, feeling frankly insulted, as I uncrossed my toes.

"All right then," he continued. "I have come across a secret colony of unusual birds which I am about to show you. You must never reveal their whereabouts to anyone. Do you understand me?"

I carefully shook my head yes, making sure not to bite my tongue, which was twisted and crossed, held down by my teeth – an old Brownie trick from my scouting days. It works exactly like crossed fingers, legally nullifying any promises. I have successfully relied upon its powers for several decades now.

"Ok, good. Let's go pishing!" he said, unlocking the doors.

Pinecraft Park is a beautiful little wooded forest like something out of a magical, tropical fairytale. There are trees of shapes and textures that most Jersey girls don't even know exist. It is positively enchanting!

I followed quietly behind my father as he made his way through the woods, stopping every now and then to pish. If you're not familiar with the birding phenomenon of pishing, you would get a kick out of seeing grown men and women making loud hissing sounds through their teeth that sound like, "pisssshhhh, pisssshhhh." They think it attracts birds. I think it attracts ridicule – as in, "people are pishing at you, not with you!"

"Pisssshhhh," my father hissed, "pisssshhhh, pisssshhhh. You hear that? They're coming!" he said excitedly.

I heard some chirping in the distance. I should probably mention to you that my father's title at Myakka River State Park is "Bird Interpreter." He is also known as "The Bird Whisperer" for his uncanny ability to communicate with birds. My mother lovingly nicknamed him "Bird Brain." He likes that.

The chirping suddenly became louder and soon a chorus of a dozen birds joined together in song. Then one by one the birds flew into sight and landed on my father's shoulders and hat. The rest gathered around his feet and on nearby branches.

"Wow!" I exclaimed at the sight. Then I noticed something interesting. Each of the birds had bands around their upper bodies. "Why are they banded?" I asked.

"They're not banded!" my father snapped. "They're bra-ed!"

"They're bra-ed?" I asked incredulously. "You mean they're wearing bras???"

"Yes, they're bra-ed!" he answered impatiently.

"Are you kidding me?" I laughed.

"Don't be so judgy!" he scolded.

"But why are they wearing bras?"

"They found some lingerie catalogs in the woods and they asked me to get them some bras."

Lingerie catalogs in the woods? Hmm, a plausible story, I thought, since my brothers were always finding Playboy magazines in the woods during the family camping trips of our youth – or perhaps hiding them there, as finally dawned on me many years later.

"So how did they get these bras?" I asked.

"They ordered them from Victoria's Secret!" he answered sarcastically. "And they call ME 'Bird Brain,'" he muttered to himself. "I had them made up, of course. I told the seamstress I needed them for my granddaughter's doll collection. I needed it to sound normal."

"Yeah, that sounds pretty normal, Dad," I agreed smirkily.

"Well, what choice did I have?" he defended. "Once these birds get something in their craw, they chirp incessantly. It's deafening!"

As if on cue, a bird in a bra flew to my shoulder and started chirping excitedly. "I'm sorry -- Yo no speak Chirpanese," I tried explaining earnestly.

"You're an idiot!" my father said shaking his head hopelessly.

"Hey, that's child abuse!" I objected.

"Hearing you say 'Chirpanese' to them is elder abuse!" he countered.

I decided to lighten the mood. "Hey Dad, what do you think these birds in bras would be worth on the blackbird market?" I joked lamely.

"A bird in a bra is worth two in a bush!" he responded begrudgingly.

The Stanley family is not known for their highbrow humor. What can I tell you?

"Enough of this nonsense!" my father snapped. "The reason I

brought you here is that they want me to ask you something. They want you to do them a favor."

"Oh, no! Absolutely not! I am NOT making parakeet panties! I refuse! I still have standards!"

My father looked hurt. "Why would they need you for that? You don't think I did a good job with the bras? Is that what you're trying to tell me?"

"No Dad, the bras are fine," I admitted.

"They don't want panties! Have you lost your mind?" he asked. "Why would these birds want panties? They're breasted and chested, not rumped and badonkadonked! I'm beginning to think you and I are not of the same species." He shook his head solemnly.

"Okay, so, what is this favor of which they peep?" I inquired. My father rolled his eyes.

"What they want is for you to take photos of them, and to start a movement -- bra-ing birds all around the world. But like I said, you must not divulge their whereabouts. Remember, you promised not to let that catbird out of the bag! They don't want creepers with peepers descending on their little colony here."

"Mmm," I responded masterfully with my trusty old non-committal sound effect.

"I happened to mention to them that you were a wildlife photographer."

"I am?" I asked surprised.

"They want you to take pictures of them -- in their bras." he added.

"But what about my reputation?" I demanded.

"What reputation?"

"Dad, I'm a wildlife photographer! Not a pornographer!"

"I only told them you were a wildlife photographer, so they'd let you meet them."

"So, I'm not a wildlife photographer?" I asked disappointedly.

My father sighed with exasperation.

"You have a great camera, you're good with the computer, just snap some pictures and it'll be fine. Will you do it for me? Will you do it for them?"

"I don't know, Dad." I shrugged.

"They want you to make a little booklet. Something that shows them off and tells their story. They say it will be the greatest thing since J.J. Audubon's *The Birds of America* and I must agree. I'm telling you, Cathy, it will be historic!" He gestured with his hands visualizing a headline in the sky, "Birds in Bras: Breasted, Chested, Boobies and Tits."

My eyes traced his hands in the air and miraculously I, too, saw his vision: "Birds in Bras..." sparkled gloriously against the cumulus clouds. Call it instinct or call it sunstroke, I heard my voice inexplicably ring out "I'll do it!"

"That's my girl!" My father beamed with pride. He turned to his flock, "She said 'Yes!'" He shouted, and pished with glee as the birds in bras joined together in song and flight.

My father looked at me and a serious expression seized his face. "There are just two stipulations: Keep my name out of it and don't give away their whereabouts!"

I quickly crossed my tongue and nodded in agreement.

And that, gentle reader, is how this extraordinary booklet came to be. I took photos of the Pinecraft Posse and made them their own little book which was a huge success! The birds in bras trend has spread like wildfire amongst the fashion-forward feathered flocks. After that, I decided to spread my wings and go in search of the best breasted, chested, boobies and tits I could find to introduce the world to this remarkable new behavioral adaptation.

So, now I'm officially a wildlife photographer, I guess. And it all started in Pinecraft Park, in Sarasota, Florida, thanks to an old ornery ornithological interpreter named Owen Stanley and his love of birds -- but you didn't hear that from me!

# # #

Golden Breasted Bunting

Blue Tits

Robin Red Breast

Brown Footed Booby

Black-Chested Jay

Marsh Tit

Green Breasted Mango

Blue Footed Boobies

Golden Breasted Starling

Lilac Breasted Roller

Red Footed Booby

White Breasted Cormorant

Tufted Titmouse

<u>Where The Boids Are</u>

<u>Black-Chested Jay</u>: Colombia, northwestern Venezuela, Panama and
    far eastern Costa Rica

<u>Blue Footed Booby</u>: tropical and subtropical regions of the eastern
    Pacific Ocean

<u>Blue Tit</u>: the British Isles and also northern Africa to Turkey

<u>Brown Footed Booby</u>: tropical and subtropical regions of the eastern
    Pacific Ocean

<u>Golden Breasted Bunting</u>: Africa south of the Sahara

<u>Golden Breasted Starling</u>: northeast Africa

<u>Green Breasted Mango</u>: the American tropics to northeastern
    Mexico

<u>Lilac Breasted Roller</u>: eastern and southern Africa

<u>Marsh Tit</u>: temperate Europe and northern Asia

<u>Red Footed Booby</u>: tropical and subtropical regions of the Atlantic,
    Pacific, and Indian Oceans

<u>Robin Red Breast</u>: (the European Robin pictured in this book) British
    Isles, western Europe and northern Africa

<u>Tufted Titmouse</u>: east of the Great Plains in the woodlands
    of the southeastern, eastern, and midwestern United States

<u>White Breasted Cormorant</u>: sub-Saharan Africa and southern Ontario

Biography

www.birdsinbras.com

Cathy Comora is the author of The Real Bitches of Sarasota & The Real Bitches of New Jersey, humorous photo/caption books about dogs, available on Amazon.com.

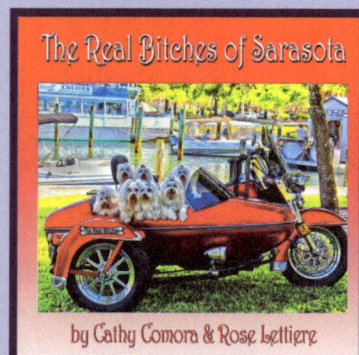

www.ingramcontent.com/pod-product-compliance
Lightning Source LLC
Chambersburg PA
CBHW041543240626
47164CB00002B/115